MW01229378

# Sarah Cass

**Paranormal Romance**

**Sarah Cass**

**www.authorsarahcass.com**

**Divine Roses Ink Publishing**

**www.divinerosesink.com**

**A Divine Roses Ink Book**
Paranormal Romance
First E-book Publication: October 2014

Leap
Copyright © 2014 Sarah Cass

Cover design by Sarah Cass
Edited by Megan Koenen
Proofread by Mary Terrani
All cover art and logo copyright © 2014 by Sarah Cass

**ALL RIGHTS RESERVED:** This literary work may not be reproduced or transmitted in any form or by any means, including electronic or photographic reproduction, in whole or in part, without express written permission.

All characters and events in this book are fictitious. Any resemblance to actual persons living or dead is strictly coincidental.

# Books by Sarah Cass

**The Tribe Series**
The Tribe
The Wolf
The Chief
The Raven
**The Dominion Falls Series**
Changing Tracks
Derailed
Dark Territory
Runaway Train
Home Signal
**The Lake Point Series**
Santa, Maybe
Deep-Fried Sweethearts
Stalled Independence
Witch Way
A Thorough Thanksgiving
Eve's New Year
Heartstrings & Hockey Pucks
Luck of the Cowgirl
Stars, Stripes & Motorbikes
Free Falling
Love for Hire
Haunted Hearts
**Stand Alone Novels**
Masked Hearts

# Dedication

To my best friend, my co-author,
my sister in spirit.
Without you I would have given up years ago.
Without you, this book wouldn't exist.
Thank you for being my bestie.

# LEAP

## Sarah Cass
## Copyright © 2014

Jayde drew the bow across the violin strings in a long, slow motion. The note resonated low and shivered through her body, as it always did. The note was familiar; it was one she'd heard playing in the back of her consciousness for weeks.

All her life Jayde had carried the magic of a Player, and that meant she could hear and Play the strings of fate that coursed through the world around her. The fate of each person in the world had its own distinctive melody, a song she could recognize and manipulate if she chose; something she only did from necessity.

She played the long, deep tenor note on her violin again, letting it mesh with the one melody she knew best of all—her own. This new fate that she heard as often as her own in the past few hours, and had become eerily familiar still managed to be elusive.

Several hours before she'd detected the shift in her own fate, and was trying to resolve the meaning behind it without success.

The violin itself wouldn't be enough for this; she had to come to terms with that and face the fate that had joined hers directly. She set aside the violin and rose, dragging the bow behind her.

Eyes closed, she focused on the magic. Around her the strings of life fell into place, each vibrating with its own ever-changing future. To the untrained Player the chords overwhelmed and clashed into chaotic dissonance. At least that's what she'd been told. There hadn't been a day she could remember that she'd heard anything but the sweet orchestral sounds that symbolized life.

According to the other Player she'd met, each Player saw the future in different ways and through different mediums. Whatever they carried in their soul influenced what they saw.

For her it was strings. Infinite, beautifully colored strings all around her, each person's set up like the neck and bridge of her favorite instrument. She even walked on them. It was hard for her to imagine how anyone could get through life not feeling, hearing, or being surrounded by the beauty of the future.

She frowned, brushing aside the stray thoughts to focus. In her right hand she still held the bow, so she raised it. Rarely did she use the bow-- her hands sufficed-- but this was a special case. Days ago she'd detected there would be yet another attempt on her life, and coincidentally that was when the new tone joined her personal melody.

She knew someone would attack her soon, and she wanted to be prepared. The next hour would be filled with split second changes to tempo and direction, along with many attempts to confuse and surprise her, so she would need to be able to find the note of her destiny amid the symphony.

With the fingers of her left hand, she strummed the threads of fate until she landed on her own. She plucked them several times as she would her violin, the pizzicato overpowering the sounds of all other fates. One last pick of the strings left the music shimmering in the air like a thousand aqua dust motes.

She lifted the bow and in one sinuous movement, played the aqua strings of her own fate. The familiar notes in the energetic tune vacillated between her own sense of peace and the apprehension of the upcoming battle. Within two bars a new, deep tone joined with hers in a rich harmony. Every note of their joined melody galvanized an exhilarating boost in magical strength. Not willing to let go just yet, she moved into a spiccato run, bouncing the bow in fast, nimble taps over the strings until she found the one the new element was tied to.

She stopped and grabbed the string, rolling her finger over it until she touched the string tied to hers. In one quick motion, she flipped her own fate's fingerboard over to find the one hidden just beneath it.

Unlike her own aqua, this was a dark midnight blue, with flecks of silver mixed in. For reasons she didn't understand, the strong new set of strings made her insides shiver in anticipation. This person would change her life.

Soon.

Her keen ears picked up a note of discord entering her personal song. She didn't have much time; she had to get to the roof where there was more room to battle.

A tiny cupboard of an apartment in New York City was no place to battle, it barely fit herself, much less the oncoming group of attackers—magical or not. She loved the city for the sheer volume of people and their songs all around her, but city-life sucked for actual living space.

She tore down the hall and shoved the stairwell door open. Below her life carried on as normal, the familiar music of her fellow tenants carried on. She chuckled. They'd never be aware of the fight to the death that would occur on the roof above them; most regular humans were oblivious to the magic all around them. When a full on battle occurred, it could happen under their noses and they'd be none the wiser.

With a deep breath, she made one last check to make sure her weapons were in place. Two sonic guns on her hips and three knives—two on her right thigh, and one on her left. The most important weapon was in its sheath on her back. The weight of her sword, Forte, was coupled with the low resonant tone it sang when it anticipated action.

Out of habit, she reached up to touch Forte's handle and the weapon sang a beautiful note in response. Yup, she was set.

Up two flights of stairs, the door to the roof already sat open. Her next-door neighbor had spent the afternoon sunbathing and failed to close it on her way back down. Jayde could still smell the sunscreen in the air.

The cool dusk air enveloped her with false promises of peace and quiet. The month old rubber surfacing on the roof masked her footsteps. Horns honked all over the city. People shouted, radios blared, and in the next building she heard a couple having a very good time in the bedroom. Some people didn't even bother to close their windows.

None of that was out of the norm, and therefore easy to tune out.

She stopped in the middle of the rooftop, turning a full circle to gauge the oncoming attackers' positions. The person that would change her fate had yet to arrive, but she'd do well enough on her own until then.

Seven magical beings ranged across the roof top in positions close enough she had reason for concern. She ran her fingers along the hilt of the dagger on her thigh, and grabbed it when the strings around her shifted and dispersed.

One of her attackers was attempting a blocking spell. Jayde laughed and spun toward the root of the spell, releasing the dagger into the dark. Before she heard the satisfying thunk of the weapons impact, she folded her knees and dropped down straight to the ground onto her back.

The hum of the oncoming spell passed right over her belly. She straightened her legs and rolled to the right, then immediately to the left. An enormous man landed where she'd just been on the rooftop so hard the entire roof trembled.

He reached for her when she hopped to her feet, and she leaped into the air to avoid the swing of his fire-powered sword. The heat of the blade reached through her leather boots. The fire-demon was sent to kill, not maim.

"Fun." She flipped over backwards, away from the demon. As she landed, she pulled out her sonic weapons. Four creatures approached, two on either side of her. Based on the notes they played on her fate, they were all Weres. The sound generated by the guns alone would disable them, never mind the physical blast from the weapons.

Practiced precision guided the weapons into the middle of each pair of thread-disruptions. She fired a round from each gun, and spun them back in to drop them in her holsters. By the time she locked them in place, all four Weres screeched into the night like banshees.

The fire-demon's red hot approach sent prickly heat up hers spine, but she waited. She pressed her hand into the strings only she could sense beneath her, and braced her feet. When the demon was inches away, she pushed off. The spring of her own magical touch launched her well over the seven foot tall demon's head.

She tucked into a ball and rolled until she landed on the cushy strings of her downstairs neighbor's fingerboard. Like a trampoline, the strings folded in under her weight and she sprung out of them gently. With another tuck and roll, she landed on the rooftop again.

Besides the fire-demon, she still had another attacker nearby whose presence was misted and muted. Only powerful magic could mute someone's presence in her future.

There were two possibilities. A powerful Sorcerer, or a Keeper. A Sorcerer would have to have intimate knowledge of Players to block her, but many used frightening means to get their magic and spells. She'd still prefer it over a Keeper. A Keeper would be bad, as attacking one could mean death.

The heat of the fire sword drew near, and Jayde reached for her own sword, Forte. It sang as it coursed through the air—from a nice leisurely adagio when she was safe, to a rapid allegro when it drew near to a foe.

The song raced through a presto pace. The heat became almost unbearable, and her fate chose that moment to pluck the chord of her future. The low note resonated under the music of her sword and all the life around her, deep and rich.

The new notes reappearance distracted her enough from the oncoming attack that fire brushed the side of her face. She hissed at the singeing pain and rolled away from the demon's return attack.

To buy a moment to concentrate, she unleashed a dagger toward the demon's face. Under his roar she found the source of the note that had become tied to her melody. Ten floors below, a negative space. Undeniably this was a Keeper.

She couldn't ponder the effect a Keeper might have on her fate; she just had to trust her lifetime of knowledge and instinct. The snarl of the approaching demon pulled her back to the rooftop.

Forte hummed in anticipation, and she obliged the sword. With a quick sidestep to avoid the demon's attack, she spun and buried Forte into his side, clean through. It wouldn't kill him, and would likely piss him off, but it would disable him for a few minutes.

She ripped the sword out and ducked under another approaching spell. Without hesitation, she stuck Forte back in its sheath and raced for the edge of the roof. The attacking spells from the distant wizard whipped past, only one grazing her, but all it did was momentarily wipe out her ability to scream.

There was no scream.

Only air.

At the edge of the roof she dove. Arms out straight until her body tilted toward the ground. Head first. Wind whipped through her hair, along her flesh, until a shatter of glass told her the Keeper knew what she was doing. She opened up her arms and the moment she impacted with his body, she grabbed on tight.

They fell for several more seconds until cold took over and she fell unconscious.

The Player remained asleep on Magnar's cot. When she'd leaped off the rooftop, he believed she knew he'd catch her. He'd been sent to protect her, but also to destroy her, although he didn't know how much her ability would let her know about his orders. By all accounts, Keepers were negative space to magic.

Their job was to protect and serve justice to magical beings, so Keepers had a dampening effect on magic. Every creature from Sorcerer, to Were, to Players, were not supposed to be able to hurt Keepers in any way; but the reverse was far from true.

The mission to destroy the Players magic took second place when he'd sensed her plummeting through the air. She'd held her own in a battle against a fire-demon, so the ballsy move shouldn't have caught him off-guard, but it had. Only thing that had shocked him more was how she'd anticipated his arrival and wrapped herself around him tight.

He'd only had seconds to collect himself and phase out of the physical plane before they hit the ground. Because of the fire demon on her tail he'd kept them phased for much longer than was good for a non-Keeper. The longer they remained in the realm between planes, the Other as Keepers called it, the more their trail dissipated.

The Other was a dark, miserable place with a magic all its own. While Keepers were, as always, unaffected, creatures of light could be deeply wounded. The Other liked to cling to light and dim its power. Fortunately for all creatures, the opposite was true of creatures of the dark. Just like magnets, when similar poles were placed close to each other, they repelled instead of attracted.

When they'd arrived at his safe house, he'd removed all weapons but her sword, which had zapped him when he'd tried to touch it. Now she lay, a tantalizing temptation, sleeping off the darkness of the Other.

Gods, she was hotter than hell. Wrapped up in leather, her body showed lean muscular lines from years of battle and training. Something someone in their mid-twenties shouldn't have. Still, she bore no visible scars.

Her skimpy top revealed enough of her stomach and back to expose a complex, intricate tattoo that appeared to wrap her entire body. He wanted nothing more than to see how much of her it covered.

In all the time he'd been a Keeper the one rule he'd followed without question was not to mate with a creature of any kind. It hadn't been a temptation until now. Unfortunately, he didn't know if his temptation was genuine, or because of the orders foisted on him.

She stirred, and then grew still. For a moment he wondered if she even breathed. Her eyes opened, revealing irises as aqua in color as the streaks in her hair. He knelt in front of her. In the years since his death he'd never met a creature like this. "Your name, Player."

"I would have yours, Keeper." Her voice carried through his cabin like a melody, and the smile she bore stirred something in him he hadn't felt in a long time—the aching need of desire.

"You leaped and expected me to catch you. I would have yours first."

"I leaped and knew you would catch me. There is a difference. However, I'll allow your stubbornness. I am Jayde."

"Magnar."

"Pleasure to meet you, Mag." She rose from the cot. Without fear, she turned her back on him and walked to the window. With her hand resting on the pane, she tilted her head. "You have us far from the world."

"We are still on Earth."

"No." Her laughter teased and tickled him.

His cock twitched at a flick of her fingers at her side, and he wondered if she played him now as he'd been warned she would. "Don't play me, Player."

"I'm not. And you misunderstood my statement. I mean we are far from people, civilization. It is rather quiet here. But we are on Earth."

"We'll be safe here."

"That's for me to determine."

When she turned and began to approach, he took a step back. "Not a good idea. You know it's best to avoid each other."

"I'm not trying to molest you, but as you're a Keeper, I must touch you if I'm to see our combined fate."

He took another step back. "You shouldn't be able to see it either way. That is what makes Keepers different."

A slow smile curved her lips and his pants grew tighter. Damn, she would be the death of him, as he was assigned to be for her in a way. He had actually been given the unusual task of ridding her of her powers, in the way only a Keeper could. To mate with a magical creature should nullify their power without killing them. Her aqua eyes scanned him from top to bottom, and she tilted her head. "How long ago did you die?"

Magnar tried not to flinch at the question. Very few knew that Keepers were once mortal, ripped from their deaths to become Keepers. Some Keepers swore it was a penance what they'd done in life, not that any of them remembered the life they'd been ripped from. "I don't remember."

"I'm guessing twenty, maybe thirty years." She took another step closer. "Do you remember what you did in life?"

"Of course not." No Keeper ever remembered their life. He found himself drawn to her, and had to force himself to back up another step. "How are you doing that?"

"I'm doing nothing." She chuckled. Despite his tension, she appeared relaxed and calm. "Don't you trust me?"

"Do you trust me?"

She paused her advance, her brows lifted high up until they were hidden by her aqua-streaked bangs. "I leaped off a fourteen-story building convinced you would catch me. I think that's the biggest game of trust ever played, dude."

"Did you just call me dude?"

"I did." Somehow in the interlude she'd managed to get inches from him. "You're a Keeper. If you have any of the knowledge of the ages Keepers are supposed to receive, you'll know that it would be punishable by death if I were to harm you. I really kind of prefer life."

He'd been given that knowledge, but then had it all blocked by his own choice. There was too much knowledge and he preferred it to come on a need to know basis. Still, even he knew the law she spoke of. He smirked. "You sure about that? You faced off with seven attackers and then leapt from a building."

"I have infinite faith in my abilities, now hush." She set her hand on his chest, right over his heart. Her eyes fluttered shut, and her features relaxed into a peaceful smile.

Goosebumps started to emerge as her breath brushed along his flesh, teasing him. Her free hand rose and the fingers on it flicked and twitched, but he felt no change within himself. He frowned, but fought the urge to ask if she was messing with him again. At that moment he wished he had some idea what she saw or felt when she tapped into the magic the way she did. He knew too little about psychics, and he had a feeling that was by design.

"You used human logic to pick this place. It's remote and discreet. To a human's eyes. To anyone with magic, we stick out like a beacon, even your negative space draws attention, and I'm like a lighthouse. We need to move."

"How fast? Can you replenish before I take you through the Other again?" The surety of her statement, and the logic of her reasoning made him trust her statement, but he hesitated to do anything that would cause her to lose consciousness again.

"I'm afraid not. We have ten minutes at best. I think it will be closer to five."

"You think?"

"In a battle, my predictions are spot on because they happen in the moment. There aren't as many possibilities ahead when you're only looking one or two seconds into the future. Once you go beyond five seconds the possibilities become infinite, depending on the choices of those involved." She still hadn't opened her eyes again, and he found himself wishing she would.

"So less than five minutes now with how long you took to explain."

"Verbosity is a gift." This time she opened her eyes and grinned. "I don't deny it."

"Then you'd best hold on."

"Oh, goody. I get to climb the tree." Without waiting for permission or instruction, she threw her arms around his neck and hopped up to wrap her legs around his waist. Then she groaned. "Crap, you distracted me. My weapons?"

"I'll get them." He wasn't about to let her down now. His duties clashed together with every second she wrapped herself around him. It wasn't unusual for him to question or disobey orders. The problem with this one was, in order to disobey he'd have to deny himself the pleasure of taking her. And denying his please wasn't something he did often.

"I know what you want to do. What you need to do," she whispered in his ear. Each light puff of air tremored along his ear and shivered down his spine. "And I still trust you. You are my fate."

Before she could say more, he grabbed her weapons and wrapped his arms tight around her. With one dark burst of magic they disappeared into the blackness of the Other. Her head dropped to his shoulder as she lost consciousness, and he lingered as long as he dared so she'd sleep a while once they returned.

If she knew he was sent to take his powers...

And still trusted him?

Maybe she knew something he didn't.

He needed answers, but he wasn't sure he wanted to hear them, either.

A great thundering rumble reverberated through the air, and into Jayde's bones. It surrounded everything around her. She slipped her hands along the world's most uncomfortable bed.

She supposed she could just ask Mag where the hell they were, but far as she could tell he wasn't anywhere around. Two trips through the Other, a lack of food, and the all-encompassing noise had her senses off-kilter something fierce. She couldn't be certain if he was nearby or not.

At last her reaching grasp was rewarded with the cold, smooth sensation of rock. No, not totally smooth. Jagged points stuck out here and there, leading her to believe it was a natural cave. Which meant the thundering was likely a waterfall, she hoped.

With a sigh, she tried to relax on the hard surface sufficing for her bed and find balance again. First, she needed to ease the pounding in her head. Using deep, regulated breaths she focused on slowing her bodies' adrenaline-fueled chaos into something akin to calm. A normal heart rate would, at the least, ease her headache.

In the midst of her descent into meditation, a disruption thumped against the familiar tune of her own fate, lending a deep resonating note to her own song. She smiled. Mag had phased back inside the cave from wherever he'd been. As she pulled out of her meditation, she could hear him shuffling around. The crinkle of paper bags, the squeak of Styrofoam, and there it was—the mouthwatering scent of food. Burgers, fries. "Bacon."

"Bacon's mine."

"Bull crap. I'm the one that's been knocked out twice. Bacon's mine."

Mag grumbled under his breath. Fortunately for him, the thundering around them, and the continuing crinkle of the paper bags covered what he said.

"Waterfall?"

"Yeah. Why?"

"Just making sure. I'm still a little off-kilter. Come here."

"What? Why?" Doubt seeped through every word. The man had issues with trust when it came to Players. She wondered what that was all about. If he even knew. There were strong spells wrapped around his strings, ones she'd be happy to remove if he allowed her to.

"Just do it, you big lug." Her reasons were two-fold. One, her senses were overloaded and the Other had mired down her magic, so she needed a magical reboot. Using the person that took her through the Other was the best way to do so. Two, she wanted him close again. Having wrapped herself around him twice in the past twenty-four hours, she knew his body felt just as good pressed against hers as the strings of his fingerboard felt wrapped up with her own.

"Why are your eyes still closed?"

She pointed to her head, "Migraine," then waved her hands around the cave. "Big noise. Two times through the Other, and battle, plus lots and lots of crazy music I can't control until I'm balanced." Okay, that last part was a half-truth, but she really wanted him near her.

"Oh, sorry." A wave of dark power expanded like a bubble around them and the physical sound of the waterfall dropped exponentially. "Can't keep that up if I'm coming and going. Now what's this about needing me for balance?"

Doubt clung to every word, but at least he was close now. When he sank onto the bed, she slid her fingers right up along his forearm. "You took me through the Other, you can help me re-focus."

His hand clamped over hers, and when he spoke, his voice was laced with tension. "Don't do that." Curiosity got the better of her and she focused on his fate. She didn't touch it, just studied the song emanating from him. Or rather, the songs. The poor man was conflicted as hell.

"It's okay. You're allowed to want me." She preferred honesty, and there was no denying he wanted her as much as she wanted him.

"No. It isn't."

"It's what you were assigned to do, drain me of my powers, yes? So, in essence, you are technically allowed to want me. You've been given express permission."

"I thought you needed balance."

"I'm getting there. Stop squirming." She gripped his arm and used the leverage to sit. Before the protest she could hear rising in his song could emerge, she gripped the back of his neck. The immediate surge of dark energy from him coursed over her flesh until her toes curled. She sighed. "That's better. Of course, I'd prefer to release that energy another way, but you're too scared of your assignment."

"Shouldn't you be afraid of my assignment?"

"Perhaps. Now let me at that food." When he moved out of her way, she climbed off what turned out to be a pallet on the floor of the cave with a few sheets and blankets draped over it. "You aren't much for comfort are you? With your power you could bring a real bed in here."

"So the mattress can get damp and moldy when I'm not here? No thanks. Now, are we safe here for a while?"

"Safe as we can be for a pair quite possibly destined to destroy each other." She grinned to lighten the moment, but it had the opposite effect on him. "Sheesh. Can't even joke about it. I didn't think you took your job that seriously."

"I don't usually. This is…different."

"Am I different?"

Rather than answer, he dug into the bag and took out more food. He set burger after burger in front of her, and three containers of fries. "There's your damn bacon. Now eat. No complaints about your figure."

"Won't get them from me. I like food too much, plus with all the people trying to kill me, I tend to keep in shape." When he dropped into his chair with a frustrated grunt, she shook her head. She sat in her own chair and draped her leg across his thigh. "Relax, happy-joy, I wasn't talking about you."

"Why do you keep touching me?"

"Fates change by the second. If I'm to make sure we remain safe, I need to keep touching you. Much as I love hearing your song, your Keeper status blocks me from our combined fate unless I touch you." She took a huge bite of her burger, and moaned low. This was no fast food burger; he'd gone to a good restaurant for their food. "This is so good."

"Didn't anyone teach you manners?" He chuckled. "Talking with your mouth full is not proper etiquette."

"Take a bite of yours, and tell me you can help from exclaiming how delicious it is." She leaned forward when he remained still. "Go on. I dare you."

Finally he tore into his burger with the crinkle of paper and an enthusiastic mouth-smacking bite. His pleasured groan shivered down her spine and she had to squirm because the mere vibration of his voice made her wet.

Goddess, she wanted him wrapped around her when they didn't have to phase. After the revelation of her knowing his assignment, he'd become more torn than ever. Such a shame, too. It would suck to know he'd been killed for not following orders. Orders she was more than happy to have him follow. She'd lived a lifetime with her powers, she could live without if necessary.

"Jayde?" He tapped her knee and even through the leather, the touch heated her flesh. "Hey."

"Hmm? Oh, right. Sorry. You were talking to me. What did you say?"

"Where were you?"

*Fucking you blind in my head, what about it?* Problem was, if she told him that he wouldn't allow her touch any longer. He'd distance himself until the necessary time. Instead she smiled and shrugged. "Just running a quick check."

"Honesty, right?"

"You know, it's easier to follow through on your orders if you seduce me."

"Do you need seducing?"

"Goddess, no. Just your voice is enough. Still, I know you aren't ready. You don't understand what you're getting into. Why is that? Why don't you know?"

He grunted and shifted in his chair. Another few lip-smacking bites of his burger muffled his next words.

"Sorry. I don't speak burger."

"Eat now. Talk later."

"Chicken."

"You need nourishment. Remember? Two trips through the void and all that jazz?"

Magnar tried to ignore the woman's grumpy eating. He didn't blame her for wanting answers, but he wasn't sure he had them all.

Her questions made him wonder at his own reasons for what he'd done, and if it was truly his own reasons. She made him question everything, including his own tendency to be a rebel against the rules of his role in the creature community.

"Oh wow." Her musical, seductive voice stirred him out of the downward spiral of his thoughts. "I know where we are now."

"Is that so?"

"This is Niagara Falls, isn't it?" She licked her fingers, and the mere sight made his cock twitch again. Damn it, was that her or his commands? When she shifted in her seat and set her foot flat on his leg, her knee bent as if she was ready to spring from her seat. "I've been here before, but it's been years. It took me a while to recognize their music; it changes as they erode the rock face."

"The falls have a song?"

"Of course. Everyone hears it, that's why they're drawn here. They feel the power, the pure force of natural magic in their song."

Euphoric. That was the only word he could use to describe the pure rapture that settled over her features when she was hearing whatever she heard around her. Clearly her magic was part of her essence, it couldn't be right to take that from someone. He cleared his throat. "I'm pretty sure it's the sight of them, they're huge."

"That's what they think it is, but you and I, we know better."

"Don't include me in your crazy."

A playful smile tweaked the corner of her lips. "You're already there, Keeper."

"Wishful thinking." Or not. He wouldn't admit to always thinking this place had music. But truthfully, it was why he'd picked it for a hideout. After a moment, he shook off his agreeing thoughts to change the subject. "There aren't many true Players, I'm told."

"That's what I'm told as well. We're as rare as core-gems. Seers are a dime a dozen, and most of them need tools like cards or stones. True Psychics, they're a little less common, but I believe the current figures are at one in every thousand creature births."

"The balance is shifting." A familiar unease settled in his shoulders until he hunched over as if to guard himself. "Humans aren't even aware of it."

"True. I've seen it coming for some time. The past few years the creatures have begun to increase in numbers, often breaking our laws to do it, without repercussion." Her head tilted as her eyes fluttered close. The burger she'd been munching on, her sixth, lay forgotten in favor of delicate, fluttering movements of her fingers.

Once again he was distracted by the idea of those touching him, or even playing him as he'd been warned she was capable of. Without stopping to think of the meaning, he touched her knee. "Is something wrong?"

A low hum slipped out of her pursed lips, the vibration of it jolted through his hand. He clenched her knee instinctively, and his eyes fell shut without his permission. Brilliant music, rapid, heated, and intense blasted through him like a rock song.

He jumped back from her touch, glaring at her even as she sat there unmoving. "What the fuck was that?"

"What?" Her fingers still teased the air; a small pucker creased her brow. "I was doing calculations. I'd say creatures are coming up on fifty percent of the population now."

"The other Keepers said you would play me."

"Trust me. If I was playing you, you'd be very aware of it." She froze and her back straightened. "What did you do?"

"What did I do? What did *you* do?" Mag rubbed his hand over his chest above his heart. The steady pulse increased its beat to match the music he'd heard.

"I told you, I was running calculations. That's all. We're now tied by two strings instead of one. How did you do that?" She rose, hands out flat with palms down. One hand skirted along the air, until a finger hooked around nothing and plucked.

Mag's gut twisted and his body jerked toward her. "You played me."

"I played myself, which isn't nearly as fun, I promise. I'd love to be played, but that's not the point. You weren't tied to that before. While I was lost, what did you do?"

"I just touched your knee."

"Well, I know that." She spun and approached. "What has you so nervous about me playing you, anyhow? You're the one that came to kill or maim me. What difference does it make?"

"I won't be a puppet on a string."

"You already are."

His limbs went numb, his stomach twisted into a stronger knot. Never mind that she'd just confirmed the fears he'd had the past few years, she knew more about him than he did. "Who's the puppet master?"

"I think you know." Her hands rested on his forearms. Even though her gaze settled on his face, her fingers traced the edges of the Celtic knot tattoos on his forearms with startling accuracy. "All Keepers are bound with magic; I've seen it too often to not notice. You, however, take it to a whole new level. Someone is trying to control you, your natural ability to rebel is making it tough, but their hold is growing stronger."

"How do you know all of this?"

"Because I'm a Player. The strings of your fate tell me many stories about your life since your death, and the lives of all around." She tilted her head, and the nerves under her fingers flamed higher. As if just her touch burned him, or the magic beneath it.

"You think I know who the one controlling me is?"

"It would stand to reason. You should recognize their magic every time you meet them, it is so engrained within you."

"It's not my boss."

"No, I don't believe it is. His spells are weak. His spells are being controlled by another Caster."

Confusion muddled his thoughts, fueled by her incessant touching, teasing his flesh and the marks on him until warmth flooded his arms into his body.

"I can almost touch it."

"That sounded dirty." He needed to distance himself now. Before he acted on instinct and did just what he'd been ordered.

"I know, but I meant your past. It's right there. I think I can get to it."

"You need to step back." Energy surged through his limbs, electric shocks followed behind her roaming fingers. "Now."

"All right." She didn't argue, just stepped a foot away. The departure of her fingers from his arms left behind only cold and residual tingles. "I think I know why you were sent to me, and I think the one trying to control you is wrong."

"It no longer matters." He couldn't follow his orders. The end result might be his own death, but the more he got to know her, the more he knew he couldn't take away what she had. The world had few Players, and he doubted any were like her. "I will rebel, as you put it, one last time."

"You can't." It was merely a whisper, but a note of panic laced her usual musical tone with dissonance.

"I must."

"You don't understand." She stepped toward him again, but he backed away. "You need to listen to me."

"No, I don't."

"Stubborn ass. You will listen. You just don't know it yet."

"I will help you hide for as long as I can. I will obey my directive to protect you from harm, and from those that have already attacked you once." He took another step back. "To do that, I must track them."

"Promise me you'll return." There was no fear, no resignation, only a stubborn lift of her chin. "I will have to take you at your word since you won't let me touch you until you've found what you need to."

"You don't know everything."

"Yes I do."

He couldn't help but respond to her teasing smile. Damn, the woman could bust his resolve with just a smile. "How do you do that?" The question spilled unbidden from his lips, but he couldn't regret it.

"What, exactly, are you referring to? There's a lot I do and do well." The low, seductive tone was back, tuning to his whole body like a pitchfork. "I'm afraid I need specifics to answer."

"You know what I've been sent to you for. You've seen every possible future for humanity, including, I'm guessing, their destruction."

"And the same for creature-kind. Do go on."

Every fiber of his being wanted to move closer, but he fought the urge. Confusion still lingered over what had happened last time they touched. Plus, if he let himself touch her again, he couldn't be sure he wouldn't follow through on his orders, and the more he was around her, the less he wanted to see her destroyed. "But you are more laid back than any creature I've ever met."

"I was born with this gift. I had it in the womb, and I'd bet most every being you've ever met has no memories of the womb like I do. When you begin life knowing everything, you either learn early how to live despite it all, or you succumb to it. I think that's why there are so few Players. It's so easy to fail to manage everything."

"I…" His heart clenched into a tight ball and surged up into his throat. There was no way to imagine what she saw all the time, every day; but her words made it easy to imagine her intense struggle. "I need to go."

"I know. Be careful." She moved toward the table and sat in front of her remaining burger. "You still didn't promise you'd return. I can't see it to be sure."

"I promise."

"And I believe you. Thank you."

Mag nodded even though she wasn't looking his way. Without another word he dropped the shield he'd raised when she'd told him of her headache and phased out of the cave. Once he was secure on dry land, he made sure a protective bubble of his own magic resumed around the cave to protect her and dampen the bright beacon of her magic.

He spun on his heel and phased again into the Other until he ended up in the one place few could go, including creatures. Rumor was even Keepers couldn't come to the core of the Earth, which meant his frequent visits left him in total privacy every time.

The earth's outer core ebbed just out of his reach from his perch near the innermost edge of the mantel. There were few that could stand the heat of the core, and he was glad for the quiet it afforded him.

Although he could sense others near, they never disturbed him, and he didn't bother to seek them out. A gem glimmered to his left, as aqua and clear as Jayde's eyes. "As rare as a core-gem, for certain."

He plucked the gem from its resting place and stuck it in his pocket. Now he just had to track the fire demon. He needed answers for Jayde more than himself now. No one deserved to be hunted, but from all he'd seen of her, she was the least deserving of such a fate.

Others with her power could easily be swayed or use it for evil. Not her.

He would save her, even if it meant his own death.

Before Mag even fully coalesced, he knew Jayde was at the edge of his protective barrier. So when he became fully solid and found her at the mouth of the cave, just inches from the brutal intensity of falling water, he wasn't surprised.

He didn't ask if she knew he was there; she was too powerful for him to doubt she knew that. Instead, he remained where he was, watching as her fingers danced over his magic.

The sun beat in through a small gap he'd created with the barrier in the falls to allow them light, and set her figure in a gorgeous silhouette. Damn, he wanted her, and she knew it too. She knew more than she should, but he trusted her more than the creature that gave him his marching orders.

"Your constant indecision is really messing with me, Mag." She broke the silence, but didn't stop running fingers along the shield protecting them from the full force of the Canadian falls in Niagara.

"You're not touching me." He frowned. She'd told him that she had to touch him to get a good vision of their combined future. It was a benefit to being a Keeper that other creatures couldn't use their gifts against a Keeper, in this case it was a detriment. They both knew his boss wanted her rendered magically inert, and Mag was the one that was supposed to disable her magic. Unfortunately, the attack at her apartment made it clear someone else wanted her dead. "So how do you know?"

"Much of you is in your barrier. It's not a perfect resolution to being able to foresee, but it works when you disappear on me." She smiled and withdrew her fingers from his shield. Her path toward him carried her in an almost glide, her feet made no noise on the rock surface. "I think you need to see something."

He wanted to back up, back away. After his journey to the core, and his chase of the fire demon, he'd been even more settled in his decision to not harm her. The fire demon had been sent by one Mag once considered a friend.

The only person he trusted now was her, even as he simultaneously feared she was just playing his strings.

She halted her progress, a frown puckered her brow. "Still going to be difficult, then? Fine. Did you find what you were looking for?"

"You already know the answer to that question."

"But I have yet to figure out if it has made you trust me more or less." She stepped toward him again. "Before you make any decisions, I have to show you something. You aren't the only one that learned things while you were gone."

When her hand settled over his heart, the betraying muscle began to beat double time. Through the curtain of her lashes he could see her aqua eyes almost spark in delight. He set his hand over hers. "Your magic won't touch me, remember?"

"If you truly believed that, you wouldn't worry about me playing you. Now hush and trust me."

He shouldn't, not after all he'd been told, but he did. With her right there, all doubt disappeared into the Other. "For now, I'll trust you."

"You are such a poor liar. No worries." She turned around and pressed her back into his chest. Her deliciously curvy ass wiggled against his cock, and he grunted. The giggle she offered in reply resonated like the brightest melody through the cave.

Without her guidance, he set his hands on her hips and leaned down to whisper in her ear. "Behave."

"I'll be telling you that soon." She lifted her arms to the sides. "Now close your eyes."

"What? No."

"Do it." This time it was a command, a power in her voice he hadn't heard before.

His cock twitched in response, and he found himself compelled to follow her orders. He closed his eyes as ordered, but kept his hands firm on her hips. "Now what?"

"Now breathe. Relax. Focus on me for a moment. It won't take you long to see."

"See what?"

"Magnar."

With a big exhale, he tried to curb his curiosity and focus on her. She pulled his focus much faster than he'd expected. The heat of her body drew him in, her soft, even breaths a whisper in the air that he swore he could now see. An aqua swirl of fireflies swooped out and danced through the air as she breathed.

"That's it," she whispered, with more than a whisper. A song, one that carried the voice of a violin. "See it all."

As the last note shimmered through the air, a cacophony of sound burst into the quiet. He flinched, almost stepping away, but instinct told him to stay still.

"Focus on me. Focus on me."

Like a beacon in the noise, her song overrode everything and he followed it. The aqua swirl coalesced into strings, stretched out before him like a guitar. One by one, strings dropped into place around them, but he stayed focused on her, afraid of being blasted by chaos again.

"Interesting." Her delicate fingers danced along the strings around them, brushing them aside and lifting her own up.

"What's so interesting?"

"It worked, and as I suspected, you have music in you. You must have carried it over from your life as a human."

"Why do you say that?"

"These are guitar strings; they are different from my strings."

"Yours are from a violin, aren't they?"

"You could have been a Player with that sort of knowledge." She strummed the strings and her tune deepened; underneath her own music a low note resonated in harmony. "You hear that, don't you? You can see it'll be difficult to lie to me here."

"I do. What is it?"

"It's you. It isn't normal for two songs to carry together. I haven't seen it in my lifetime. Not like this. When people walk similar paths, it looks like this." She brushed aside several fingerboards and lifted a pair that was layered one on top of the other.

He dared to lift his fingers from her hips and ran them along the sets of strings. "The songs, they're different. They run the same path and are compatible in many ways, but they're different."

"Those two are married, mated Weres. They were destined for each other and there are still variances in their songs." She pushed them aside to once again lift her own beautiful song. With a deft, swift movement, she flipped it over to reveal a dark midnight blue set of strings with flecks of silver. The song was almost identical, and the sets of strings would only move together.

He strummed the strings and a jolt ran down his spine.

"Easy, big boy. If you don't know how to play yourself, it can be overwhelming at first. Take it slow."

"That's me?" He frowned and wrapped his arm around her waist, pulling her flush against him. "It's like that because we are close."

"It was like that before you got me horny as hell breathing in my ear with your hot breath, Mag." She chuckled; her body trembled against his and made his own body far too aware of their extreme proximity. "I shouldn't have known you were coming. Most Keepers manage to surprise the hell out of me, but I knew you were there."

"You also knew I'd catch you." He didn't release his tight hold on her, but reached toward their strings, his and hers.

"That's it." She slid her hand down his arm until their hands met at their strings. "This shouldn't be."

"Did someone do it? You said I'm being controlled. Could someone have done this, then?"

"No. No one can do this; I can't even force them together. This is why you were brought to me. Why you've been manipulated into doing something you both want to do and don't want to do. You would have shown up in my life, orders or not. It's only the orders and the fear of what will happen if you follow through that makes you so conflicted. You are supposed to be here, with me, a part of me."

"I might have had a lot of the Keeper's knowledge bound, but even I know that Keepers and creatures can't mate. It would leave you alive without your magic. In some cases it could even kill you."

"So?" Unbelievably, she shrugged. "I suppose it would take some getting used to, but I've been gifted with this my whole life. If it had to go away, I would survive. It's certainly not my only magical gift."

"I couldn't take this from you."

"There's a good chance you won't." She ran her fingers down their strings one last time before she pushed them back into the sea of strings around them. "But we'll discuss that once you are free of the spell."

"I don't want to be." With their strings pushed into line with the rest of the world's a veritable concert of sound, along with a museum of artful colors filled their space. No longer was it an unbearable cacophony, but more like an intense rock concert full of guitars and violins he could get lost in.

"It's intoxicating once you're used to it. Your music tastes mesh well with mine." Her fingers laced with his, and she leaned into him as he rested his chin on her head. "What did you find?"

"You're going to ruin it."

"Just stay relaxed, it's not going anywhere. Tell me what you found."

"Fingal sent the fire demon."

"Fingal, the albino?" Once again her fingers trailed along his tattoos, even as her gaze remained on the entrance of the cave.

"Yes Fingal the albino, who I once considered my friend until our different views on humans became too much. I've known him for many years. As long as I can remember. I think it was his sorcery that was used to bind the knowledge for me."

"There are many that wish there were no psychics of any nature in the world."

"I can guess why."

"Can you?" The pace of her finger trails along his tattoos increased, a burning fire of nerves rising in her wake. "It is not Fingal. He has a cruel, but specific goal he doesn't want me to see. It's someone else that's bound you, and they have worse plans."

"Jayde."

"Plans for the end days."

"Jayde." Magnar tried to pull his arms from the magical dance of her fingers, but they were locked in place by her simple touch. Whatever spell she was weaving, he was the source. He couldn't begin to comprehend how the burning pain was becoming far too distracting for clear thoughts. "*Jayde.*"

"End days," she whispered. The symphony around them sped up, strings flying by until it felt like a special effect of warp drive on a sci-fi show.

Magnar flinched when all the strings exploded, discordant notes screeched through the cave, and fire overwhelmed them until dissipating into nothing.

With the steady, even rush of water pouring outside the cave the quiet resounded around the room, and the burning in his tattoos eased. Jayde became heavy in his arms, and he dared open his eyes to find her bent over them unconscious.

When he touched her arm, the flesh was cold to the touch. If he couldn't detect her life with his magic, he might have thought her dead.

"Jayde." He pulled her to standing just long enough to scoop her into his arms. Without hesitation he laid her on the pallet bed and climbed in next to her.

As he wrapped his arms around her to hold her close, he tried to convince himself he was just helping her get warm. Deep down, he knew it was far more. His inner conflict hadn't eased one bit, and grew worse. Something told him she'd do everything in her power to sway him one way or the other.

He'd just have to be stronger than her.

If that was at all possible.

"I know you're awake." Mag's statement edged on a complaint.

*Damn.* Jayde hoped he'd remain ignorant for some time. She rather enjoyed lying flush against him. Her leg draped over his waist, her ankle resting against a rather impressively firm ass.

"You are back in the land of the living; have been for some time. Maybe we should separate before it's too late."

*It's already too late.* She sighed against his neck. "Want to see something cool?"

"What?"

The distraction was intentional, allowing her to remain wrapped in his warmth a while longer. With a smile she tilted her head back. She focused on the idea of the color purple until magic tingled along her scalp and eyes. His gasp let her know he'd seen the change, but she added the bonus of opening her eyes for him.

"They change?"

"Whatever color I want. I went orange for a while, but my orange eyes disturbed far too many people. Aqua seemed a safer bet." She tilted her head into his hand when he ran his fingers along the streaks she knew now shimmered purple. By all accounts, her eyes always matched the streaks in her hair.

"Reason?"

She giggled. "Well aren't you prolific this morning. Not a morning person?"

"Not on a morning after you've nearly died in my arms, no." He pinched her side. "Now do you want to talk about it or your hair?"

"It's been like this since I was born. My adoptive parents were mere humans, but very open to creatures and accepting of what I was. Their family, not so much. Since the streaks won't dye away, we dyed the rest of my hair brown instead of blond and I kept brown eyes until I was old enough to 'rebel'." She led her fingers on a slow crawl up his chest. "Except in times of distress, I am always in control of the color."

"I prefer the aqua."

"As you wish." After a moment of concentration, the tingle returned and she smiled when he relaxed some. "If you really want to know about last night, you were there. You know what happened. There's something about our connection that makes the future possibility of total annihilation more intense."

"Gee. That's flattering."

She giggled, and the giggle took over until her head fell back in full-on laughter. "I just meant it's tied to the person attempting to control you, is all. You do make everything more intense for me, though. That's something I'll never complain about."

"Jayde," he whispered against her lips before she could actually kiss him. "I can't hurt you. I won't."

"You won't."

"You said yourself you don't know that."

"You don't want me hurt, but what will happen if we don't give in? You'll be recalled against your will. Tortured and possibly meet final death – meanwhile they'll send someone to me to finish the job you couldn't—and by force."

"I'll protect you." The fierce growl of his voice was accentuated by the tightening of his arm that pressed her firmer against him.

"I think the solution is in following your orders. I can't be certain, no, but I think you were meant to come into my life long before you were magically manipulated into it."

"What do you mean?" His grip relaxed, and he leaned toward her. The hard planes of his body stretched along the length of her, keeping her pressed into the pallet and assuring her his body was more willing than his mind.

"No one has ever been able to partake in my Player abilities, even fellow Players. No one, Mag. Our connection goes beyond anything that can be manipulated. I told you, nothing I've ever experienced compares."

"What if you're wrong?"

"Then I know you'll protect me from what consequences I face. Should I lose my ability, there will be other things to deal with, but it's a chance I'm willing to take. I've lived with my ability my whole life, I won't live without ever seeing what this is, and I wouldn't be able to live knowing I caused your death."

His fingers brushed along her cheek in a gentle touch that stirred her down to her soul. "What about the price you're asking me to pay?"

"I'm asking you to have faith. In my ability, in my instincts, and in the Goddess herself." She slid her fingers down his spine, and as she did all other destinies faded into the Nether, leaving just hers and his entwined. With one pluck of her finger, his cock twitched against her hip.

"Jayde." He groaned, nuzzling her neck. "Don't manipulate me."

"I'm not. Just teasing you." She smiled and nipped at his earlobe. "Same as if I did that. Play me, Mag. I've never been Played."

"What?" He pulled back enough to leave a dousing of cool air between them. "Won't that mess with the future?"

"I thought you realized by now, being a Player is more than being a psychic. You have to Play with intention. You can only change the future if you will it. Otherwise, you can strum the strings to your heart's content and not affect a thing unless you want to. If you want to play someone, really play them, you must do so with intent."

"How…" His words faded into a moan as she laced her fingers into his hair and willed him to see the fates. This time her strings became a guitar neck that he could easily play, while his became a violin for her nimble fingers. He strummed her strings in a gentle rhythm that sent a soothing vibration through her. "Are you sure?"

"Please," she whispered.

He plucked a string with one finger, and a jolt went right to her clit. His low chuckle broke through her moan as he nibbled on her neck. "I think I like this."

In response she only plucked one of his strings to tease him right back. She arched into him when he bit down on the sweet spot in the crease of her neck.

Then he began to play in earnest, each pluck and strum of his fingers teasing along her flesh, through every nerve ending in her pussy right to her g-spot. The melody was intense, hot, and built to a peak only to slow down moments before her release.

He teased a slow trail of kisses up her neck and nibbled along her jaw line. "Turn it off. It's time for the real thing."

She stuck her lip out in a pout. "But I was enjoying that."

"You'll enjoy this too." To her great pleasure, he accentuated the promise with one last pluck of the strings.

She cried out as the tremors swept through her, whimpering when it ended too soon as he set his palm flat against the strings. "Tease."

"No I'm not."

Without further hesitation she brushed away the magic, leaving them surrounded only by each other and the constant rumble of water outside the cave. "Prove it."

He trailed his finger down along her throat and continued along her breastbone until he got to her leather halter-top. Inch by inch he unzipped the leather; each vibration teased her erect nipples until she squirmed with impatience.

The moment the zipper was undone all of her clothes disappeared in a cool-aired touched of magic. She might have complained, but the brush of cold against her hot flesh made her shiver in all the right ways.

When she set her hands on his shoulders, she was thrilled to find he'd helped his own clothes off at the same time. Before she could form a compliment, he captured her lips in an intense kiss.

His tongue swept through her mouth, teasing her with promises of more. He broke the contact far too soon, only to lip, nip, and suck his way down her neck. The moment he sucked her nipple into his hot mouth her pussy clenched and she dug her nails into his shoulders. She was rewarded with a delicious growl that added vibration to his suction, and he followed it up with a bite.

Too soon, but not soon enough, he continued his trail down her body. He teased along her stomach with light touches, and the tickling heat of his lips. As his tongue swirled around her navel, he gripped her thighs and spread her legs wide.

She bit her lip and her hips jerked when he slid his thumb through her folds, grazing her clit, teasing her entrance before pulling away. A soft whimper accompanied her pout. "Gods, Mag…"

He slid his hands down her thighs and parted her folds. Cool air slipped along the sensitive, inflamed flesh before he swept his warm tongue through her heat. She gripped the sheets, fighting the urge to tease him with magic.

One of his long fingers penetrated her entrance, and with all the skill he used Playing her, he stroked her passage. He added a second finger as he sucked her clit into his mouth, nipping on the sensitive nub.

Her body trembled at the waves of pleasure coursing through her with every touch, and harsh bite of his teeth. The pleasure built until nothing existed but his touch.

She twisted the blankets in her hand, then released them to bury her fingers in his hair and held on for dear life. Moments away from her climax, with every one of her nerves on fire, he backed off. An embarrassing whimpering cry echoed through the cave when he pulled back. "Goddess, you're cruel."

His low laugh did little to ease her grumpiness as he crept up along her body. Flesh against flesh, every inch of his touch was pure torture without her release. He positioned himself just right to press the tip of his cock against her entrance. "Grumpy, little Player?"

"Please, Mag. Don't tease me." She clasped her hands around his neck, trying to pull him closer. Her legs wrapped around his waist, she wanted so much more.

"The first time I bring you to orgasm, you're going to be trembling around my cock, not my fingers. Understood?"

"Is that a promise?"

Instead of answering, he drove his full length into her hard and fast. Her body stretched to accommodate him, and she tightened her legs around his waist in a desperate urge to pull him even deeper.

He withdrew slowly, until she whimpered again. When she raked her nails along his shoulder, his back arched and he moaned. "Fuck, Jayde."

"Please do." She squeezed her legs and lifted her hips so he was shoved deep inside again. When his mouth descended on hers, she met him eagerly.

His thrusts were no longer slow, and she met his fevered passion with her own. Like he was made for her, every stroke hit her G-spot until only fireworks of light filled her mind and she couldn't have found their strings if she tried.

She clung to him, her hips rushing to meet his until he gripped her ass and lifted it to alter their position. Her back arched to meet his demands, and she was rewarded with him teasing her clit until she couldn't hold back any longer.

With a keening cry, she let the orgasm sweep through her. Her muscles clenched around him, and her whole body shook in response. Just as the tremors began to ease, he grunted and his hard length pulsed inside her.

He lowered himself enough to capture her lips again in a slow, sensuous kiss. She reveled in the warm planes of his mouth as they clung to each other.

Just as they began to fully settle, and relax into comfort, a loud note of music filled her senses. Combined violin and guitar strummed through the cave, and them, filling her with another orgasm she sensed mirrored in him. She gasped out of the kiss, and he buried his face in her neck as he shuddered above her.

He kissed her jugular and muttered, "I thought I told you to put it away."

"That wasn't me. It was us. Instead of two strings joined, there are now three. We became more connected than we were before." She couldn't stop her smile. "It's all so clear now. I didn't understand before."

"What?" He pulled her close and rolled to the side. One finger trailed along her shoulder, then down her arm. The tender touch promised much more, and she hated to break the mood with her revelation.

She smiled and shook her head. "It's nothing that can't wait. I want to enjoy our night until we're exhausted and must sleep."

"What about your powers, they're still there right?"

"For now. The Keeper's touch saps the power, drains it slowly. It will be morning before we know anything for certain. So please, let us enjoy the full range of pleasure while we know we can."

"The change in our connection doesn't help you see anything further?" Concern darkened his tone, even as he kissed her shoulder and brushed his thumb under her breast.

"Nope. We'll know in the morning, and I don't want to talk about it." She cupped his cheek and lifted his lips to hers. "I just want to enjoy this and deal with the consequences in the morning, if there are any."

"I'm still worried."

"I know. You're also still a man."

"Good point."

Magnar didn't sleep a wink. Exhaustion dragged at his eyelids, but he refused to let them close. Every moment Jayde slept was an eternity of concern bordering on panic. He waited for anything, any sign that he'd stolen her vitality and power with his complete lack of restraint.

Even knowing he might have, he couldn't regret what had happened the night before. He'd had his share of women, but none had been anything like Jayde. If he wanted a cop out he could say it was because those women were human, and he'd never been with a creature for the exact reason he was now worried for Jayde.

He didn't want a cop out. Something told him this was more than that, and her words from last night fueled the belief. *'It's all so clear now. I didn't understand before.'*

Everything went back to her power, to their threads of fate that were bound in a way she said she'd never experienced before.

Another big boost to his belief was her total, absolute trust in him. Before they'd ever met, she'd leapt off a building confident he would catch her and take her somewhere safe. He was a Keeper. She shouldn't have known he was even there, but she had.

"It's really difficult to sleep when someone is staring at you like some creepy stalker dude in one of those angsty teen novels so popular these days." The familiar and beautiful smile lit her features before he was granted the gorgeous aqua sparkle of her eyes. "Before you ask – it's still there. Nothing has faded at all. I'm fine."

"That doesn't make sense."

"Well I'm happy too." She snorted and smacked his chest. "We'll find the answers."

"Are you sure?" He leaned his elbow on the pillow next to her head and rested his cheek on his fist. "There's a shitload of questions going through my head right now."

"You aren't alone in that. I think it has to do with what the one that wants to control you didn't anticipate." Her hesitation didn't help the unease still twisting his stomach.

"Tell me. It's worse to see you nervous."

"I'm just not sure how you'll take it. I mean, I'm pretty sure you'll be alright, but there are a few possible futures where you aren't."

"Jayde."

"We're mates."

Confusion won over the shock, and he furrowed his brow. "I thought that only happened among the animal-kind. Old instincts, or whatever."

"That's usually true. You must have something in you that was there before you died and returned as a Keeper. They usually take humans as Keepers, so maybe it's a distant part of your blood line." She shifted closer to him, an efficient distraction.

"You're adding more questions with every answer you give me, Player." Despite his confusion and doubt, he felt compelled to ease her nerves at his response. "So we are mates, I know basically what it means, but you showed me Were mates, and they weren't like us."

"I know. That's something only the Goddess can answer, I think. There must be a reason we are bound down to our very souls and songs. It may have everything to do with freeing you from your manipulators, or it may be more than that."

"No one will be happy this didn't work. My boss, the one trying to control me, the other Keepers."

Her brow creased and she laced her fingers with his. She pulled them tight against her chest. "I know. The first thing I must do is free you of the spell that compels you to return on command. I didn't risk my own magic only to lose you again."

"Can you do that?" He ran his thumb along her brow and the crease relaxed away. "I didn't think Keeper spells could be changed."

"I don't know. I'm certain I can ferret out the spell, but actually removing it will be tricky, and most likely won't be comfortable for you." Her fingers brushed along his arm, pausing briefly over his tattoos before returning to his hand. "It will be like that with every spell I must remove."

"I can handle pain." He lifted their entwined hands and kissed the back of hers. "I trust you as you trusted me."

She eased back into a smile, a very welcome sight. Damn if he wasn't falling hard for her—maybe this mate thing wasn't so far off. With a sigh, she settled into the crook of his arm. "There is much to do. We won't be able to stay anywhere too long, but we have to return to my apartment."

"We can't. They'll be waiting for you."

"Shit. But I need my violin. It was specially made for me, I need it." She worried her lip between her teeth. "I can get my spell casting tools anywhere, but the violin and the bow itself are a necessity."

"I'll get them for you. How long until we have to move this time?"

"We might have two days, but the sooner the better."

He thought for a minute. "You'll always want to be somewhere with people, which will leave us to major metropolises around the world, tourist traps, and the like."

"It would be best. I'll try to keep the powers to a minimum, but when I'm working on you, it'll be a good blast of power." She shrugged. "I prefer cities anyhow. The more music the better."

"I'm thinking New Orleans next. I have a safe house there I haven't used for years. It'll be safe for a short time, I think."

Her fingers danced in the air for a few moments before she nodded agreement. "New Orleans will work. There's excess magic there anyway from the overflow of creatures and humans attempting magic."

"First you'll remove the spell for my recall."

"Then we'll work our way through the rest of them, one by one." She nodded. "We also need to find out who is trying to control you, who wants the Players dead."

"Can you find the other Players? We need to warn them, don't we?"

"Yes." She took a deep breath and tried to sit.

He wasn't about to let her go just yet. With one hand he stopped her motion and pushed her back onto the pallet. He pressed his body into hers, reveling in her soft curves and smooth skin. "Say it again."

Her brows puckered into a 'V'. She set her hands on his biceps. "Say what?"

"Tell me again what you realized last night."

A grin teased the corners of her lips. "You already know what I realized."

"I want to hear it again."

"Maybe I want to hear you say it."

He lowered down until his lips brushed her ear. The tremble of her body beneath him got his cock twitching, and his balls tightened with need. "We're mates."

"Yes," she whispered against his ear.

"That means lots of sex."

She laughed. "Pig."

"And more."

After a sharp intake of breath, he could feel her nod. "Much more."

"We're more than mates."

"Yes. I think we are bound. I don't know if our final string will bind or not, but I think it will." Her fingers laced into his hair, nails scraped his scalp. "And then we will be one."

"Shall we try to bind them now?"

"Yes."

Jayde leaned on the railing, her eyes closed and magic at a minimum. With her powers turned down she could focus on the normal, everyday hum of activity around her. Tourists gasped at the sight of the falls, locals grumbled about tourists, the powerful thunder of the water poured over the edge into the pool below.

They'd spent too much time at Niagara. Afterglow and the realization of their destiny as mates despite their disparate roles in the creature world had kept her and Magnar snug in his private cave beneath the powerful force that was the Canadian falls.

Footsteps passed to the right and left, but her ears picked up one set carrying on a steady beat. The hum of her body was beyond magic as he drew near. She smiled as he pressed his body against hers. "Did you get everything?"

"Your violin is safe, nestled near my guitar at our next destination." His voice strummed her nerves as his breath brushed her ear. "Just as you are safe near me."

She curved back against him, to make sure her ass brushed him seductively. "I'm safe until you're distracted."

"Even then," he whispered. "I'll protect you more fiercely."

"Where to next?"

"New Orleans." He wrapped his arm around her waist. "We'll stay in populated areas until we're sure of the plan, but even there we'll have trouble."

"I'm ready for battle. Always have been. The question is, are you ready to fight what you didn't know was the enemy?"

"I don't like that you think it's a Keeper." His arm tensed around her waist, the seductive note in his voice hardened into anger. "I hate rules, but even I would never betray the rule that we are here for creatures' protection. Not their destruction."

"It only makes sense. They're masked to me. With the exception of you, all Keepers are but mere shadows to my senses." She sighed when a shift of the wind brought the cool mist of the falls toward them.

"Can you tell what's ahead?"

"I know our lives will be in danger."

His warm chuckle carried through her body. "I could have told you that."

"We will have moments of joy."

"I like that."

"But beyond that the future is too uncertain. Everything changes, including our future." She laced her fingers through his.

"As long as you have my back in battle."

"And you have mine."

"I'll take the unknown."

# *The End*

# About the Author

Sarah Cass' world is regularly turned upside down by her three special needs kids and loving mate, so she breaks genre barriers; dabbling in horror, straight fiction and urban fantasy. She loves historicals and romance, and characters who are real and flawed, so she writes to understand what makes her fictional people tick. And she lives for a happy ending – eventually. And enough twists to make it look like she enjoys her title of Queen of Trauma Drama a little too much.

An ADD tendency leaves her with a variety of interests that include singing, dancing, crafting, cooking, and being a photographer. She fights through the struggles of the day, knowing the battles are her crucible; she may emerge scarred, but always stronger. The rhythms to her activities drive her words forward, pushing her through the labyrinths of the heart and the nightmares of the mind, driving her to find resolutions to her characters' problems.

While busy creating worlds and characters as real to her as her own family, she leads an active online life with her blog, Redefining Perfect, which gives a real and sometimes raw glimpse into her life and art. You can most often find her popping out her 140 characters in Twitter speak, and on Facebook.

http://authorsarahcass.com

# Books by Sarah Cass

**The Tribe Series**
The Tribe
The Wolf
The Chief
The Raven
**The Dominion Falls Series**
Changing Tracks
Derailed
Dark Territory
Runaway Train
Home Signal
**The Lake Point Series**
Santa, Maybe
Deep-Fried Sweethearts
Stalled Independence
Witch Way
A Thorough Thanksgiving
Eve's New Year
Heartstrings & Hockey Pucks
Luck of the Cowgirl
Stars, Stripes & Motorbikes
Free Falling
Love for Hire
Haunted Hearts
**Stand Alone Novels**
Masked Hearts

# Divine Roses Ink

Made in the USA
Columbia, SC
09 September 2024

42038023R00035